Peacock Fan

Pam Scheunemann

Illustrated by Neena Chawla

Consulting Editor, Diane Craig, M.A./Reading Specialist

Published by ABDO Publishing Company, 4940 Viking Drive, Edina, Minnesota 55435.

Printed in the United States.

Credits
Edited by: Pam Price
Curriculum Coordinator: Nancy Tuminelly
Cover and Interior Design and Production: Mighty Media
Photo Credits: Corbis Images, Digital Vision, iStockphoto, iStockphoto/Christina Craft, iStockphoto/Christopher Ho, iStockphoto/Helen Koshkina, iStockphoto/Ogen Perry, ShutterStock

Library of Congress Cataloging-in-Publication Data

Scheunemann, Pam, 1955-
    Peacock fan / Pam Scheunemann; illustrated by Neena Chawla.
       p. cm. -- (Fact & fiction. Critter chronicles)
    Summary: Famous movie star Pierre Penny, whose films include "101 Peacocks" and "Bye-Bye Birdies," meets his number one fan. Alternating pages provide facts about peafowl.
    ISBN 10 1-59928-460-X (hardcover)
    ISBN 10 1-59928-461-8 (paperback)

    ISBN 13 978-1-59928-460-6 (hardcover)
    ISBN 13 978-1-59928-461-3 (paperback)
    [1. Fans (Persons)--Fiction. 2. Actors and actresses--Fiction. 3. Peacocks--Fiction.] I. Chawla, Neena, ill.
  II. Title. III. Series.

    PZ7.S34424Pef 2006
    [E]--dc22   2006005548

SandCastle Level: Fluent

SandCastle™ books are created by a professional team of educators, reading specialists, and content developers around five essential components—phonemic awareness, phonics, vocabulary, text comprehension, and fluency—to assist young readers as they develop reading skills and strategies and increase their general knowledge. All books are written, reviewed, and leveled for guided reading, early reading intervention, and Accelerated Reader® programs for use in shared, guided, and independent reading and writing activities to support a balanced approach to literacy instruction. The SandCastle™ series has four levels that correspond to early literacy development. The levels help teachers and parents select appropriate books for young readers.

Emerging Readers
(no flags)

Beginning Readers
(1 flag)

Transitional Readers
(2 flags)

Fluent Readers
(3 flags)

These levels are meant only as a guide. All levels are subject to change.

FACT & Fiction

This series provides early fluent readers the opportunity to develop reading comprehension strategies and increase fluency. These books are appropriate for guided, shared, and independent reading.

FACT The left-hand pages incorporate realistic photographs to enhance readers' understanding of informational text.

Fiction The right-hand pages engage readers with an entertaining, narrative story that is supported by whimsical illustrations.

The Fact and Fiction pages can be read separately to improve comprehension through questioning, predicting, making inferences, and summarizing. They can also be read side-by-side, in spreads, which encourages students to explore and examine different writing styles.

FACT OR Fiction? This fun quiz helps reinforce students' understanding of what is real and not real.

SPEED READ The text-only version of each section includes word-count rulers for fluency practice and assessment.

GLOSSARY Higher-level vocabulary and concepts are defined in the glossary.

SandCastle™ would like to hear from you.

Tell us your stories about reading this book. What was your favorite page? Was there something hard that you needed help with? Share the ups and downs of learning to read. To get posted on the ABDO Publishing Company Web site, send us an e-mail at:

sandcastle@abdopublishing.com

Peafowl are one of the most colorful birds,
especially the males.

Pierre Penny is a famous movie star. He has starred in such films as *101 Peacocks* and *Bye-Bye Birdies*.

Pierre's phone rings. It is his manager. "Yes, I'm doing the spot for Rainbow Paints today," Pierre says. "I need to leave in a few minutes."

The male peafowl is called a peacock. The female is called a peahen, and the babies are called peachicks.

Mara is Pierre's biggest fan. She is always trying to snap photos for the official Pierre Penny Fan Web site. She dreams of actually meeting him. Her friend Ellen always teases her, "You wouldn't even know what to do if you did meet him!"

Both male and female peafowl have a crest of feathers on their heads.

Each day, on her way to work, Mara passes by Pierre's apartment building. She longs for a glimpse of her favorite star. Today she sees him. "Oh, my goodness," she gasps. "There he is!"

9

Peafowl make loud honks and shrieking noises when danger is near or when courting.

Before she can take a picture, Pierre is whisked into a waiting limo. "Please wait, Pierre! I'm your number one fan!" she shrieks. Pierre turns his head, but the limo takes off.

11

Peafowl come in a variety of colors, including blue, green, white, light brown, and purple.

Mara is heartbroken that she missed Pierre, but she must hurry off to work. She works in the advertising department of Rainbow Paints.

13

Many parks and zoos allow peafowl to roam freely around the grounds.

When Mara arrives at work, her boss says, "Mara, I need you to supervise the shoot for our new TV commercial. The studio is just across the street."

Peafowl fly only short distances, usually to escape danger or to roost on a tree branch.

Mara is still feeling a bit gloomy,
having once again missed getting
a photo of Pierre. She grabs her bag
and trudges to the studio.

The peacock has long, ornamental feathers with eyespots on the tips. When courting, these feathers are displayed like a fan.

When she gets into the studio, who does she see but Pierre Penny! Her heart pounds so hard she almost faints. Pierre greets her warmly and says, "I'm sorry I couldn't stop for a picture this morning. Let's take one now." Not only does Mara get her photo but Pierre asks her to be in it with him! Mara can't wait to tell Ellen.

19

FACT or Fiction?

Read each statement below. Then decide whether it's from the FACT section or the Fiction section!

  1. Peafowl use telephones.

  2. Peafowl make loud honks and shrieking noises.

  3. Peafowl come in many colors.

  4. Peafowl pose for pictures.

Peafowl are one of the most colorful birds,   8
especially the males.   11

The male peafowl is called a peacock. The female is   21
called a peahen, and the babies are called peachicks.   30

Both male and female peafowl have a crest of   39
feathers on their heads.   43

Peafowl make loud honks and shrieking noises   50
when danger is near or when courting.   57

Peafowl come in a variety of colors, including blue,   66
green, white, light brown, and purple.   72

Many parks and zoos allow peafowl to roam freely   81
around the grounds.   84

Peafowl fly only short distances, usually to escape   92
danger or to roost on a tree branch.   100

The peacock has long, ornamental feathers with   107
eyespots on the tips. When courting, these feathers are   116
displayed like a fan.   120

Pierre Penny is a famous movie star. He has 9
starred in such films as *101 Peacocks* and *Bye-Bye* 19
Birdies. 20

Pierre's phone rings. It is his manager. "Yes, 28
I'm doing the spot for Rainbow Paints today," 36
Pierre says. "I need to leave in a few minutes." 46

Mara is Pierre's biggest fan. She is always trying 55
to snap photos for the official Pierre Penny Fan 64
Web site. She dreams of actually meeting him. 72
Her friend Ellen always teases her, "You wouldn't 80
even know what to do if you did meet him!" 90

Each day, on her way to work, Mara passes by 100
Pierre's apartment building. She longs for a 107
glimpse of her favorite star. Today she sees him. 116
"Oh, my goodness," she gasps. "There he is!" 124

Before she can take a picture, Pierre is whisked 133
into a waiting limo. "Please wait, Pierre! I'm 141
your number one fan!" she shrieks. Pierre turns 149
his head, but the limo takes off. 156

22

Mara is heartbroken that she missed Pierre, but she must hurry off to work. She works in the advertising department of Rainbow Paints.

When Mara arrives at work, her boss says, "Mara, I need you to supervise the shoot for our new TV commercial. The studio is just across the street."

Mara is still feeling a bit gloomy, having once again missed getting a photo of Pierre. She grabs her bag and trudges to the studio.

When she gets into the studio, who does she see but Pierre Penny! Her heart pounds so hard she almost faints. Pierre greets her warmly and says, "I'm sorry I couldn't stop for a picture this morning. Let's take one now." Not only does Mara get her photo but Pierre asks her to be in it with him! Mara can't wait to tell Ellen.

164
174
179
187
198
207
216
225
232
242
251
259
269
279
291
296

GLOSSARY

court. to try to attract a mate

crest. the upright, decorative feathers on top of a bird's head

escape. to get away from someone or something

eyespot. a round marking that resembles an eye

gloomy. feeling sad and hopeless

roost. to sit or sleep on a perch

shriek. a shrill cry

spot. a short commercial or presentation

trudge. to walk in a slow, heavy-footed manner

To see a complete list of SandCastle™ books and other nonfiction titles from ABDO Publishing Company, visit www.abdopublishing.com or contact us at: 4940 Viking Drive, Edina, Minnesota 55435 • 1-800-800-1312 • fax: 1-952-831-1632